The Eleventh Hour

A Curious Mystery

Graeme Base

A book is read, a story ends, a telling tale is told.
But who can say what mysteries a single page may hold?
A maze of hidden codes and clues, a clock at every turn,
And only time will tell what other secrets you may learn . . .

INVITATION

Dear --------------

Please come to my Fancy Dress Party
and help celebrate
my 11th Birthday
on
11th November
at
My Place.   Horace.

For Robyn
And for my parents

Viking Kestrel

When Horace turned Eleven he decided there should be
Some kind of celebration. 'For my friends', he said, 'and me.
For though I've been the age of eight and nine and six and seven,
This is the very first time that I've ever been Eleven!'

With that he set to work and wrote the name of every Guest,
And then eleven sorts of food that Elephants like best.
He wrote the Invitations next (and sent them off that day),
And finally eleven Games for everyone to play.

Now Horace was a clever lad; he planned the day with care,
Ensuring that his party would be quite a Grand Affair.
But only in the Kitchen was his genius unfurled,
For Elephants are verily the best cooks in the world.

He started off with cheesecake full of strawberries and cream,
Then moved on through the pastries to a Chocolate Supreme.
And though it may be said, perhaps, that Horace made a mess,
The Feast that he created was Fantastic, nothing less.

'Twas early in the morning when the Party Guests arrived
And each was wearing Fancy Dress most artfully contrived.
The Pig came as an Admiral, the Zebra as a Punk.
The Rhino was an Astronaut, his spacesuit made of junk.

The Swan arrived as Princess Pure, a most enchanting sight,
Bejewelled with rows of precious stones and dressed in purest white.
And with her came an Indian, with arrows, spear and bow –
A handsome Bengal Tiger, whom no one seemed to know.

The Mouse came as a Musketeer, his head and hat held high,
A swagger in his footsteps and a twinkle in his eye.
The Cat was Cleopatra, Queen of Egypt and the Nile,
And, masquerading as a Judge, was Sam the Crocodile.

And then there was a pair of twins – two sisters, both Giraffes,
Who turned up dressed as Angels and received a round of laughs.
Their haloes shone upon their heads, two shiny golden rings,
And from their nylon tutus sprouted painted cardboard wings.

The Guests were met by Horace as they stepped into the Hall
(He'd dressed as a Centurion of Rome Before the Fall);
And once inside they looked around and noticed with a smile
The way the Hall had been designed in High Renaissance style.

No sooner had they entered than a rumour filled the air,
And stopped the conversation as the news spread everywhere.
Their Host had made a Banquet! It was huge! Immense in size!
And one by one the Guests were drawn within to feast their eyes . . .

For there upon the table was The Feast That Horace Made,
A wondrous spread of cakes and buns and jugs of lemonade.
And in its midst a Centrepiece of Grand Design was placed,
That left no doubt young Horace had superb artistic taste.

But if the Guests had hoped to eat the Banquet there and then,
They soon found out their Host had plans for what they'd eat and when,
For Horace told them firmly not a crumb would they devour,
Until the time that he had set – THE ELEVENTH HOUR.

The Games began at 8.05 – a sack-race marked the start,
With sacks of every size and shape, so everyone took part.
They set off at a cracking pace, with Eric to the fore,
But close behind the others hopped, on trotter, hoof and paw.

They raced across the Croquet Lawn, then up towards the house,
But as they reached the half-way point the Pig tripped on the Mouse.
He landed with a heavy thud, and several others fell,
But Kilroy kept his balance, and went on to win, as well!

The Ballroom was the venue for the second party game,
But though the rules were simple no one seemed to know the aim.
They charged around a ring of chairs beneath the chandeliers,
While Sam played Mozart's 'Magic Flute' and 'British Grenadiers'.

And one by one the chairs became just piles of splintered wood,
(The Guests were all agreed that this new game was jolly good!)
Then as the final chair collapsed they stopped and checked the score;
And since no one had won at all, they settled on a draw.

The Pig procured a pack of cards and soon a game began.
But unbeknown to all the rest the Admiral had a plan,
For Oliver won every trick; his conquest was complete.
A string of luck? Or could it be the porker was a cheat?

A little later in the day some Guests played Snakes and Ladders,
Upon a board that squirmed and turned with Pythons, Asps and Adders.
The board was set, the race was on, the game had just begun,
Then Thomas went and ate the dice, so no one ever won.

A Cricket Match was organised for those who knew the game –
The twin Giraffes had no idea, but fielded just the same.
But Oliver, a Boastful Pig, had made it understood
That when it came to batting he was really rather good.

The Tiger donned the keeper's gloves and crouched behind the stumps,
And waited for a chance to show his skill at leaps and jumps.
The Pig went for a mighty swing, but only clipped the ball,
And Maxwell leapt, and caught him out. Pride comes before a fall.

The Cricket Match had finished when the Zebra took his cue
And challenged tiny Kilroy to a game of Pool or two.
But Kilroy's skill was quite immense for somebody so small –
Though Eric thought he'd win hoofs down, he didn't pot a ball.

The other Guests enjoyed a lively game of Blind Man's Buff,
With Piggy in the Middle (you would think he'd had enough!).
He blundered blindfold round the room and groped and grabbed and gripped,
While all the others squealed with joy, and dodged and ducked and dipped.

A Tennis Match was under way a little later on,
With Crocodile and Tiger versus Elephant and Swan.
The Elephant was shaky: it appeared he'd lost his nerve.
The score was 40/30 with Crocodile to serve.

Sam tossed the ball into the air then struck it with such force
That Horace didn't see it start upon its fateful course,
And sure enough it hit poor Horace square upon the head.
'Game, Set and Match', the Tiger cried. 'That's life', poor Horace said.

And meanwhile, midst Egyptian columns, row on silent row,
A Seeker searched while others Hid – a game that all will know.
But though her eyes were large and bright, the Cat's success was small,
For while she searched with utmost care, she found no one at all.

And far above, upon a hill beyond the Tennis Court,
The Rhino and the Zebra sat in silence, deep in thought.
They studied every Rook and Pawn, each King and Queen and Knight,
Then both agreed it looked too hard, and quit without a fight.

The final game was Tug o' War – two teams of equal weight –
But every mind was on the feast, the time was getting late!
The Rhino slipped, the game was lost, they cared not in the least!
For finally the Hour had come – 'twas time to eat the Feast!

'My friends', said Horace to his Guests, 'my friends, lend me your ears!
For now it is that I, your Host, have reached Eleven years!'
But if he planned to make a speech, his virtues to espouse,
He missed his chance, 'coz everyone took off towards the house!

They raced each other up the stairs (Eleven steps in all),
Then past the marble statues leading to the Banquet Hall.
And there they stopped. No body spoke. They stood in disbelief.
For all the food had disappeared. Aghast, they cried: 'A Thief!'

The cakes had turned to scattered crumbs, no cream was to be seen,
And nothing now remained where once the Chocolate Mousse had been.
The Centrepiece had toppled, not a strawberry was left.
'But who', they cried, 'could possibly have managed such a theft?'

The Zebra said, 'It wasn't I!
By All my Stripes, I'd rather die!'
The Tiger said, 'It wasn't me!
I've far too much integrity.'
Then Cora cried, 'It wasn't us!
We wouldn't dare cause such a fuss.'
And Kilroy squeaked, 'I'm far too small;
One mouse could never eat it all!'

The Swan looked darkly at the Pig,
'The Thief must be someone who's big!'
But Oliver denied all guilt,
And said, 'Now Thomas, he's well built.'
The Rhino sobbed, through sniffs and tears,
'I've known our Host for years and years,
And though my appetite is large,
I must deny this dreadful charge.'

With manners fine or poise uncouth, ~ Yea, all who seek take heed forsooth, ~ For everyone has told the truth!

The Cat had yet to say a word,
Which Eric thought could be inferred
As Prima Facie evidence
Of Feline Guilt *re* this Offence.
But Alexandra lashed her tail,
'Your theories are to no avail!
We Cats do *not* steal others' food.
It's wicked, bad and *very* rude!'

The Judge was next: 'I too deny,
Although I have no alibi,
All blame for this horrendous crime . . .'
(He waffled on for quite some time.)
'I'm not the kind of Crocodile
To fake a tear or force a smile.
My countenance is plain to read;
My friends, I did not do this deed!'

The Mystery was Curious! The Guests were at a loss,
But Horace had initiative; he showed them who was Boss.
'The Feast is gone, we can't change that, but now it's clear to see
That what we need is cheering up – just leave it all to me.'

He rushed into the Kitchen and was gone for quite a while,
Then re-emerged with sandwiches, a flourish and a smile.
'This lot is not as fancy as the Birthday Feast', he said,
'But eleven times as healthy, 'coz it's made with wholemeal bread!'

Then, as they sat and ate their lunch, there came one last surprise,
When Horace asked for everyone to kindly close their eyes.
And there it was – the Birthday Cake! The Guests all clapped and cheered.
He'd kept it in the Kitchen, and it hadn't disappeared!

And so they picnicked on the lawn until the evening fell,
And everyone left satisfied – the day had finished well.
But in the end, although the thief was someone they all knew,
They never found out who it was that stole the feast – can you?

THE THIEF WASS OMEO NET HEY ALLK NEW

Notes for Detectives

With a little close observation and some simple deduction it is quite easy to discover which of the eleven animals stole the feast. Look carefully at the pictures, and when you think you know who it was, use the first letter of that animal's name to decode the panel below.

Here's what to do. If you think the thief was, say, Maxwell, then call 'M' the letter A, and go on through the alphabet so 'N' equals B, 'O' equals C and so on. In this way you can decode the hidden message below, which will tell you who stole the feast and, more importantly, how it was done.

MYXQBKDEVKDSYXC ! SD GKC SXNOON USVBYI
DRO WYECO GRY CDYVO DRO POKCD. LED RO
RKN ROVZ : YXO REXNBON KXN OVOFOX YP
USVBYI'C PEBBI BOVKDSFOC RSN DROWCOVFOC
SX DRO RYECO KXN KBYEXN DRO QKBNOX KXN,
KD OVOFOX WSXEDOC DY OVOFOX DROI KVV
CMKWZOBON SXDY DRO LKXAEOD RKVV GSDR USVBYI
KXN KDO EZ KW YP RYBKMO'C LOKEDSPEV PYYN.
KXN XYG, TECD DY CRYG RYG MVOFOB IYE KBO,
MKX IYE PSXN YXO REXNBON KXN OVOFOX WSMO
RSNNOX SX DRO ZSMDEBOC? RKZZI REXDSXQ !

Viking Kestrel. Penguin Books Australia Ltd, 487 Maroondah Highway, PO Box 257, Ringwood, Victoria 3134, Australia.
Penguin Books (N.Z.) Ltd, 182–190 Wairau Road, Auckland 10, New Zealand.
First published by Viking Kestrel 1988. 10 9 8 7 6 5 4 3 2
Copyright © Doublebase Pty Ltd, 1988

Typeset in Palatino by Meredith Typesetting Pty Ltd, Melbourne
Transparencies by Latrobe Colourlab, Melbourne
Colour separations by CS Graphic Reproduction Pty Ltd, Melbourne
Printed in Australia by Owen King Pty Ltd, Melbourne

Produced by Viking O'Neil, 56 Claremont Street, South Yarra, Victoria 3141, Australia, a division of Penguin Books Australia Ltd
Cataloguing-in-Publication data
Base, Graeme, 1958–
The eleventh hour.
ISBN 0 670 82325 2.
1. Elephants – Juvenile fiction. I. Title.
A823'.3